This book is dedicated to

Robert Keith Reed

A friend for life

Preface

Tones of Emotion is a collection of short stories that I wrote in the form of rhyming poems based on a variety of subjects that include personal experiences, well-known events and mere expressions of my imagination. Some are humorous and uplifting and some are inspirational while others contain elements of tragedy and pain—all intended to strike a broad range of emotional tones.

While writing another book, I needed a poem to serve as a lead-in to one of the chapters. Unable to find one that was suitable, I decided to venture out and write one of my own. My effort resulted in the creation of **A Friend for Life,** a poem about a dear friend who contracted a fatal illness and after spending years mounting a courageous fight, was finally taken away. Writing it was difficult, but it served as an emotional release for me and began my experimentation using rhyme to accentuate the emotional impact of a story. The personal fulfillment I received from writing the first one led me to write others until, before I knew it, I had amassed the collection I've assembled here.

Each story is preceded by a brief introduction that tells you what inspired me to write it and provides some background to help minimize ambiguity. When reading verses authored by others, I'm often left dazed and confused as I attempt to decode the message that is clearly outside of my realm of understanding. **Tones of Emotion** is a collection of simple stories told by a simple man.

Contents

Chariots of Thunder 1

Angel in Paradise 5

Beauty Queen 11

Cobra 15

Daddy's Girl 19

Dinner for Two 23

A Friend for Life 27

Little Brother 31

Love Child 35

The Magnifying Glass 37

A Sailor's Tale 41

The Beach 49

The Bench 53

The Soldier 57

Treasured Chest 61

The Mirror 65

The Runt 69

The Western 73

Cyber Date 77

Chariots of Thunder

The 1960s and '70s marked an era of fast cars, street racing and the desire by some to "rule the road" with automobiles sporting powerful engines, big tires and ridiculously poor gas mileage. **Chariots of Thunder** describes an actual event that took place one evening on a country road just outside of Brandon, Florida in the summer of 1971. Also on board were my girlfriend Darlene and my best friend Keith.

Our 1966 Mustang, though rough-looking on the outside, was fitted with a few high-performance components that made it a "sleeper," a "wolf in sheep's clothing." Cruising down a long stretch of road one night, we passed a carload of local kids in a hoodless Ford Torino stopped at a side-street. They engaged in pursuit, and appearing to be easy prey, they challenged us to a race. We were left with no choice but to defend our honor through a display of automotive superiority. It's what we lived for—it's what we did!

Keith was driving, I was riding shotgun and Darlene was perched on the center hump. As the Torino attempted to pass, Keith went into an adrenalin-based panic and started yelling for instructions, "What should I do!" I told him to "nail it!"

The rest is history.

Chariots of Thunder

Back in the day before the EPA when the streets were ripe for plunder,
there were drivers bold who ruled the road in their Chariots of Thunder.

For me and the gang it was a souped up 'stang that looked a little bit rough,
but looks - no need, she was built for speed, she was more than fast enough.

With a faded crown of chalky brown, she was easy to ignore,
bald tires beneath, but the heart of a beast and a four-speed on the floor.

Cruising along a country road one humid summer night,
the full moon's glow was enough to show a fast approaching sight.

An old Torino without a hood was coming up from the rear,
she carried a crew, a clueless few with faces that showed no fear.

They couldn't see what would never be—to beat us in a race,
with a gambler's pride they pulled alongside and tried to up the pace.

I warned aloud that they had no chance, that they'd best be on their way,
or choose defeat "cause you will be beat, no mercy for you today!"

Driving a steed of similar breed their gestures were simply rude.
I said, "Here's the deal, see how it feels to be turned into Mustang food."

"We'll chew you up, spit you out and leave you in our dust,
so bring it on if you're feeling strong, we'll spank you if we must."

Like desperadoes face to face and both prepared to draw,
he hit the gas and tried to pass—for us it was the final straw.

I yanked her back into second gear and could hear the bald tires screech,
a lesson learned, they'd soon be burned, we were way beyond their reach.

My girl Darlene let a high-pitched scream as our rubber gripped the road,
and away she went—to the back seat sent as we jumped into "racing mode."

I could feel their dread as we pulled ahead and shot into the night,
'twas then they knew not a thing they'd do could keep them in the fight.

That car could go! What a knockout blow, just to show them who was boss,
we'd end the duel and hand the fools a humiliating loss.

Again the 'stang had done us right, the race was clearly won.
Man, what a ride! We were high on pride for the damage we had done.

They caught up at last and drove on past while acknowledging defeat,
I did feel bad since they looked so sad to be so badly beat.

I flashed my lights as they pulled away, just a gesture of good luck.
"If you want a rematch let me know, I'll bring my pickup truck."

Those days of old with drivers bold and laws much less severe,
when to be outpaced and lose a race was the greatest thing to fear.

Side by side they race with pride, their egos on the line,
a sacred need to win with speed and victory so divine.

They still exist but must resist lest a racer's fate prevail,
the fine will cost, insurance lost, might even go to jail.

Some will try to fly on by, a racer's spell they're under,
so either hit the gas or let 'em pass in their Chariots of Thunder.

Angel in Paradise

I wrote **Angel in Paradise** after reading Beth Holloway's book, **Loving Natalee**, about the tragic disappearance of her daughter on the island of Aruba. I wrote this poem in the first-person perspective since my view of the events was derived from Beth's own words. It was my intent to capture the emotion surrounding Beth's desperation and grief as she dealt with the horrific ordeal of having not only lost her daughter, but of having to deal with one obstacle after another while she mounted a courageous search for answers.

Angel in Paradise

The dawn of day, I wake and pray I'm living in a dream,
I've cried for years, a million tears, sometimes I want to scream.

I leave my bed for a task I dread, the contents of her room
I'll pack today, we'll move away, it's happening all too soon.

It's hard for me when all I see is what she left behind,
to take a look and close the book, but she'll not leave my mind.

A sacred place, my baby's space where purple is the rule,
upon the door, the robe she wore her final day in school.

A heavy heart, just where to start, her room sits undisturbed,
to still not know, I miss her so, it all seems so absurd.

An endless game, but who's to blame, and where's my daughter gone?
The hurt won't go, I need to know who'd do my girl so wrong.

Her curio, the first to go, inside—her treasures lay,
it's there because her friends from Oz would need a place to stay.

Her closet rack, so neatly stacked, her wardrobe hanging still,
the pain it brings, her favorite things, the boxes I must fill.

Of all her shoes, the ones I'd choose, of ruby red they'd be,
her heels she'd tap and in a snap she'd be back home with me.

I still replay that fateful day the journey would begin,
a tale to tell, a mother's hell, the life I knew—would end.

Some things to do, to rendezvous at a house not far away,
"Now you take care and please beware", the words a mom would say.

"Just watch your back, remain a pack, you'll be safe, guaranteed,
you're still a child, no running wild, be diligent, take heed."

We checked her list, her cheek I kissed, with duffle bag in hand,
then up the walk, no time for talk, they'd make the flight as planned.

I'll not forget her silhouette as she disappeared from view,
the last I'd see of my Natalee, if only then I knew.

I'd planned to be with family, the ones I seldom saw,
some time to take, beside the lake in Hot Springs, Arkansas.

Just us three, my friends and me, would take the day-long drive,
to get some sun and have some fun, forget the nine-to-five.

The house was packed, we joked and laughed, was such a pleasant stay,
a festive mood, delicious food, but came the final day.

Time to leave, a yellow sleeve around somebody's drink,
in letters green, were words I'd seen that made me stop and think.

Why the lure, I'm not quite sure, a sign it had to be,
my heart would race, I knew the place and I feared for Natalee.

A trendy bar in a land afar that Aruban tourists grace,
my biggest fear, she'd not stay clear of **Carlos and Charlie's** place.

A sense of dread, our goodbyes said, that trip would take its toll,
a distant stare, a time for prayer, "Please God, protect her soul."

But worst of all, I got a call, in Memphis, Tennessee,
and then I learned, my fears confirmed, the worst had come to be.

My phone would ring, the words would sting, "Your daughter didn't show.
She'll miss the flight, was gone all night and where, we just don't know."

I couldn't feel, but took the wheel, the pedal to the floor,
a high-speed ride to my daughter's side, I could think of nothing more.

My mobile phone was set to roam, a private plane we'd found,
my tear-stained face, a somber place, but at last—Aruba bound.

The flight was brief and filled with grief, the questions in my mind.
Along the way, I'd think and pray, my baby I must find!

That paradise was not so nice, an isle of rock and sand,
and there to greet, just wind and heat, an unfamiliar land.

On the ground we gathered 'round, the search would start real soon,
the Holiday Inn, where we'd begin, we'd start in Natalee's room.

At last it came, a person's name and a car that was painted gray,
his name, "Joran," a local man, on girls he was known to prey.

They'd chance to meet, just up the street at **Carlos and Charlie's** bar,
and like a shark, intentions dark, he took things way too far.

They'd drink and talk, from friends she'd walk—then off into the night.
It hurt to know they'd let her go and not put up a fight.

His dad, a judge who wouldn't budge, no matter what he'd done,
some answers sought and back he fought, "You'd best not answer, son."

Some video would let us know if Joran's words were true,
that Natalee had been set free, but my suspicions grew.

We did our best, we made requests, surveillance tapes to see,
as hard we tried, access denied by their security.

Officials there just didn't care, "We're sure she'll turn up soon."
A simple shrug, "It's likely drugs, she's in a choller room."

"Everyone knows everyone", the phrase I often heard,
I felt inside, the facts—they'd hide, some wouldn't say a word.

So hard I tried, so many lies, deceit was all around,
a mother's plea, another lead, we ran them all to ground.

But I'd not tire, internal fire would keep me going strong,
the need to quell a mother's hell, I ran so fast, so long.

The island's side they hoped to hide, our search would take us to,
to find my girl, an underworld that tourists never knew.

For profit sake, the kids they take, they rob and make them stay,
and local cops don't make them stop, they look the other way.

From door to door, we searched some more, was danger all around,
despite my fear, I made it clear, my daughter will be found!

The TV crews that cover news made sure the world would know,
to bring us clues, some interviews I did on cable shows.

The story grew and Aruba knew, some facts they would contain,
the tourist trade might start to fade with their reputation stained.

The pressure on, before too long my light began to dim,
I needed hope to help me cope, I needed help from "Him."

So hard I prayed, no progress made, a test of faith indeed,
but why would he abandon me in my greatest time of need?

To touch her hair, to be right there, to see her one more time,
the choice I'd make, her place I'd take, I'd trade her life for mine.

My spirit low, no place to go for me to be alone,
perhaps a priest I'd need to see, so tired of life I'd grown.

No longer numb, the pain would come, a rush of falling tears,
"Oh God," I'd plead, "Your help I need, where do I go from here?"

A taxi ride, the countryside, upon a cross we'd come,
and up the hill were others still, I kneeled at every one.

As I arrived at number five, an answer from above,
a sense of peace came over me, God told me of his love.

"Your Natalee is safe with me, you have no need to fear,"
I'd do my best, resume my quest, my vision now was clear.

Still we'd fail to find a trail, such grave despair and dread,
then eye to eye, the FBI said, "Beth, she may be dead."

From the start, deep in my heart, I knew the chance was there,
but all my hope went up in smoke, his words were hard to bear.

The mission changed, 'twas now remains beneath a burial plot,
to search I would, but bad or good, a rescue, likely not.

The legal scene would gather steam when Greta came to town,
her skill would prove she'd make things move, that's why FOX sent her down.

She took her crew to van der Sloot, the dad she'd question more,
he'd start to crack from our attack, his sweat began to pour.

Day to day, what they would say would only contradict,
I'd so despise the constant lies, small chance that they'd convict.

To local folk, was such a joke, deception showed right through,
but our support was growing short, was nothing I could do.

Our island home had turned to stone, our welcome not to be,
no longer friends, the search would end, the suspects all set free.

Was time to leave my Natalee and make the journey home,
a better place, in God's embrace, her spirit free to roam.

So hard to go, but of my soul, I'd leave a part behind,
and on the way, I hoped, someday my baby I would find.

No more rage, I'd turn the page and chart a different course,
to educate for safety's sake, a passion-driven force.

I made a choice, I'd be the voice and make my daughter proud,
to please beware and tread with care, my message clear and loud!

I swore that day, if I had my way no parent in the world,
would have to do what I went through when I lost my little girl.

Sometimes at night I'll look up high, beneath the full moon's glow,
and hope by chance, I'll see her dance along the yellow brick road.

For eighteen years her hopes and fears were such a part of me,
the life she'd live, so much to give, my darling Natalee.

Beauty Queen

Like **Angel in Paradise**, **Beauty Queen** is based on events that took place before and after the tragic loss of another of America's youth—JonBenét Ramsey. Most of my research came from a book that was written shortly after the incident, entitled "Death of a Little Princess" by Carlton Smith. Beauty Queen chronicles some of the events that took place as the search for a suspect ensued. Though I make reference to the widely-held view that promoting young girls through beauty pageants can have potentially harmful side effects and may have contributed to the tragedy, I believe that Patsy's intentions were only those of a loving mother who had a positive personal experience in the pageant scene and wanted her to have the opportunity to capitalize on her God-given beauty.

Beauty Queen

At an early age, she took the stage, her mother was her guide,
such poise and grace, an angel's face, her parents' love and pride.

To all of those who'd watch her pose, a talent they would see,
a natural smile, a sense of style, a model she might be.

The pageant scene could yield a dream, young daughters on display,
so cute, so small, but viewed by all, mixed messages conveyed.

To some not clear, those little dears in such risqué attire,
a suggestive pose, too much exposed—might spark a dark desire.

Opponents claim, their folks to blame who do their children wrong,
at great expense, their innocence just might not last as long.

Before a wife, young Patsy's life was filled with pageant fare,
a beauty queen when just a teen, success she chose to share.

A Southern Belle, she knew so well that benefits could come
to those bestowed a beauty's glow, a gift enjoyed by some.

Raised in faith, good mother's trait, her girl she'd help succeed,
to train her well so she'd excel, a loving mother's need.

Succeed she did, a special kid, so many titles won,
a prodigy the child would be, her future just begun.

A time to pause as Santa Clause would soon be dropping by,
as she might say, her favorite day, a happy-family time.

Christmas day would fade away as evening came to call,
a busy day for JonBenét, then off to bed for all.

The break of dawn as Patsy yawned, the first to leave her bed,
a pot to brew, a task she knew, a path she'd often tread.

But not this day, for on the way, a letter she would see,
a yellow page with words of rage, then pages two and three.

A ransom note that someone wrote—"we have your little girl,"
and a tragic play would start that day, the stage would be the world.

More words of dread, it also said, "some cash you have to bare,
don't try pursuit, we'll execute, a call—you'd best not dare."

A dream it seemed, but Patsy's scream would bring John down the stairs,
their daughter's room, they'd learn too soon, their baby wasn't there.

A search ensued to look for clues, how did they come and go?
No broken glass, no way to pass, no footsteps in the snow.

Beset by gloom, from room to room, John looked for any sign,
an opened door, the cellar floor, a sight no dad should find.

On tile of clay, his daughter lay, so quiet and so cold,
beneath a sheet, eternal sleep, a baby six years old.

A horrid scene, no cries or screams were heard by them that night,
a precious child, an act so vile, an undetected plight.

So filled with grief and disbelief, he took her in his arms,
and up the stairs, profound despair, "who'd do our baby harm?"

Those words of sin by Sharpie pen, a distraction meant to be,
as later found so cruelly bound, a cold and heartless deed.

Christmas night, by colored light, that house became a hell,
events took place, of grave disgrace, and why—no one could tell.

The media and FBI on Boulder would descend,
be friend or foe, so soon they'd know the meaning of "defend."

Neighbors, cops, the local shops, they all had things to say,
a story told, a product sold, few facts to cloud the way.

The public's sleuth, the tabloid's truth, from sources they would hide,
sordid plots, crime scene shots and quotes from those who lied.

The world resorts to open court when facts are in short supply,
some need no truth to prosecute despite a blinded eye.

The mystery was still to be as months would turn to years,
so much time, an unsolved crime, and countless fallen tears.

The world would learn, another turn in a well-known tragic tale,
as Patsy's life had added strife when her health began to fail.

Ten years passed, so long harassed, her time to be at rest,
to see her girl in the after world, God's gift, to be so blessed.

Two years more would pass before they cleared the family name,
that fateful day that DNA would redirect the blame.

JonBenét looked down that day, her mother at her side,
for only she would hold the key to what took place that night.

Will truth be told? What the future holds, no one can truly say,
but a beauty queen did reign supreme and does so to this day.

That precious face will hold a place in hearts around the world,
it's JonBenét whose name will stay, that gorgeous baby girl.

Cobra

Even thirty years after my experience in Chariots of Thunder, I never lost my love for muscle cars from the vintage years of the sixties and seventies. An iconic example of the day was the AC Cobra, a vision of the infamous Carroll Shelby—racing legend and creator of the Cobra brand. In the early 1960s, Shelby was in need of a car he could use to challenge the Chevrolet Corvette and a host of European entrants in the Le Mans automobile races.

At the same time, a small British car manufacturer that produced the "AC Ace" lost its source of engines when the company that manufactured them went out of business. Carroll decided to import a couple of cars and fit them each with a new Ford V-8 engine. So was born the ***AC Cobra***. As he marketed the cars to the American public, he would change their colors frequently so it would appear that a larger number of cars existed. The color of legend became Guardsman's Blue with white racing stripes.

By 1967, the appearance of the more aerodynamic **Coupe** marked the end of the AC Cobra's reign. But the iconic shape of the original car has led to the creation of a huge replica market with numerous manufacturers producing clones of the famous car.

Cobra

I never got bored with my souped up Ford and some quarter-a-gallon gas,
the things I did as a '60s kid when I felt like going fast.

Showing our might from light to light, the sound of squealing tire,
proving who's boss with a loud exhaust just bellowing smoke and fire.

But then, like now, most all would bow to the sign of a coiled up snake,
and the story be told of a vision bold, as history one would make.

A little car from a land afar, was about to lose its heart,
when a man in black and a cowboy hat would give it a fresh new start.

"Back in the day", as the old guys say, "That Shelby did it right,"
and Hans and Franz from track Le Mans would finally lose the fight.

He bought just two, painted one blue and added some stripes for looks,
and Carroll's name soon became the subject of countless books.

They both had a date with a little V-8 and would join the FIA.
Ferraris and 'Vettes would lose all bets when Cobras came to play.

But the glory was brief, for like a thief, the big blocks stole the stage,
"Get the tools, we'll show those fools, it's time to turn the page!"

Like a gift from heaven, the 427 became the magic word,
with a nip and tuck, and a bit of luck, Mr. Shelby produced "the Turd."

A beauty not, she ran real hot, they'd chop, bend, twist and hack,
with a big block sound and race track bound, the Shelby team was back!

The same cute face, but a whole new race, so many trophies won,
that big V-8 would seal their fate, a legend they'd become.

There was no escape, that curvy shape, a captivating style,
like a valiant steed, she'd hit top speed in about a quarter-mile.

As they say, she'd have her day, but all good things must end,
for winning's sake, we must innovate or the lead we'll not defend.

She couldn't meet the need for "sleek" and the Coupe would soon debut,
but the Cobra's reign had won her fame and her legend only grew.

Years would pass, but then at last, like a Phoenix from the flame,
a glass remake of a famous shape would restore the Cobra name.

Vintage bold, though not so old, a replica they say,
but oh so real—the look and feel, with parts from modern day.

An industry would come to be, as makers sold their kits,
and Snakes galore from shore to shore would give old Shelby fits.

Any show where Cobras go, they'd garner such appeal,
but such dismay when lookers say, "Is that a kit or real?"

The words "kit car" could leave a scar on some of the owners' pride,
but new or old, they'd trade their soul for a chance to take a ride.

A day of sun can yield more fun than a Cobra man can take,
but whatever you do, be sure that you don't call his car a fake.

She may not be from sixty-three, but to him she's solid gold,
a vintage heart, some modern parts, and smiles a hundred fold.

Daddy's Girl

In the story, **Daddy's Girl**, a young couple decides to conceive a child against the recommendation of their doctor. Despite the warning, they continue their attempt to have a baby. Finally their prayers are answered with the birth of a little girl.

Though born premature, she grows into a beautiful, loving child who is very close to her dad, an active duty soldier. All her life, she harbored a physical defect that wouldn't become known until after the occurrence of a tragic event.

Daddy's Girl

They felt such dread when the doctors said "A child you'll never bear,"
your family tree, a damaged seed, an act you shouldn't dare.

The risk denied, so hard they tried and finally got their way,
when darling little Alice came on a joyous summer day.

They'd cheated fate, an early date, so frail and premature,
though small in size, a parent's prize, so innocent and pure.

Seven years would come and go, a beauty she would be,
a love for nature, mom and dad, a spirit young and free.

No one knew why she never grew, so delicate and small,
not like other kids her age who'd grown up strong and tall.

A tiny frame, a golden mane and eyes of liquid blue,
the angels' choice, a whispery voice as soft as morning dew.

Alice was a daddy's girl and always by his side.
"My daddy is an Army man," she'd tell her friends with pride.

But drums of war on a distant shore would call her dad away,
a soldier proud, a cheering crowd, a price he had to pay.

The sky was stained with clouds and rain on the day that he'd depart,
though proud she'd be, to see him leave would only break her heart.

Looking clean in fatigues of green he hugged his little doll,
"Now you be good and mind your mom, I'll see you in the fall."

He breathed a sigh as he waved goodbye, his tears he couldn't hide,
so long a stay, to be away from his baby and his bride.

She waved and squeezed her teddy bear she'd had since she was two,
a present from her favorite dad, the little bear named Boo.

Every day, the mailman came, a note she'd hope to find,
a written kiss from the dad she missed, to know she's on his mind.

He wasn't gone for very long when tragic news arrived,
his men he saved as battle raged, but bravery took his life.

With broken heart beyond repair, her health began to fail,
her youthful glow would shine no more, her body growing pale.

Wrapped so tight in a gown of white and little Boo close by,
for days she'd wait to learn her fate, her mom right by her side.

"We suspect a heart defect"—her mother's greatest fear,
the news was bleak, her heart so weak, the end was growing near.

"Alice is to be released, there's just no need to stay,"
he promised that a nurse would come to visit every day.

Her mommy asked, "What can I do to make my girl feel better?"
She thought a while and then she smiled, just read me daddy's letter.

A Mom and daughter lay in bed all snuggled side by side,
she read the note, the words he wrote while both broke down and cried.

The sixth of May, her final day, awakened from a dream,
a wingless angel by her side all dressed in Army green.

A soothing and familiar voice said "Alice, time to go,
your daddy's here, no need to fear, I've come to take you home."

Dinner for Two

Dinner for Two came together one evening when the wife and I couldn't reach an agreement on a restaurant that would serve our drastically different moods. The fact that I've spent the last twenty-five years of my life traveling the world and sampling a wide variety of cuisine helped me formulate this story. It's a little bit bizarre, but then, so am I.

Dinner for Two

Friday night, the wife and I were ready for a treat,
our cupboard bare, was nothing there, "Hey, let's go out and eat!"

For me the need was beans and cheese, but hers was garlic pork,
her choice to be where you sip hot tea and eat without a fork.

Now I don't care for Chinese fare, for me it's chips and dip,
"Hold the tea, a Corona please," that's all I want to sip!

So I took a look in the yellow book in search of common ground,
to my surprise, before my eyes, the perfect spot I found.

A place nearby we'd failed to try, the perfect ethnic blend,
bean-based goo and egg rolls too, both palates they'd attend.

A drive not far, behind a bar was a door obscured from view,
and overhead a sign that read, "The Taco-Fu-Manchu."

Once inside, we went by guide to a table in the back,
the waiter came and gave his name, "they call me Taco Mack."

Said, "Lucy Ling was from Beijing and chose to be my wife,
a restaurant we both would want, to have a better life".

"I had to sell my Taco Bell to get the cash we'd need,
an Asian fare with Latin flair, our place—unique indeed."

"Furthermore, the wall décor was painted there by hand,
a Shanghai night beneath moonlight, on the shores of the Rio Grande."

Prepared to dine, but on my mind, an apprehensive thought,
the menu came, some crazy names, like none I'd ever bought.

I can't recall a time at all, when a taco filled with horse,
or tongue of yak with Monterey jack was offered as a course.

A note I read on the menu said, "no Beano needed here,
and powdered rat contains no fat, no heart attack to fear."

I got my chips, but in the dip, as I began to stir,
a little piece of greasy meat and little tufts of fur.

A bit unnerved by the food they served, I chose one sure to please,
but when it came, it seemed quite strange, "that doesn't look like cheese!"

The rice looked nice and I took a bite, but not my kind of food,
the wife just said, "don't lose your head, you're going to kill the mood."

About that time, it came to mind that all about the place,
no single guys, romantic eyes, all gazing face to face.

Just couples there with lovers' stare, a few began to dance,
I looked around, there was no sound, just dancers in a trance.

'Twas then I knew that in the food were herbs supplied by Mack,
that peppered taste and been replaced with an aphrodisiac.

"The spice we use is nothing new, an ancient recipe,
it flavors food, but sets a mood for every lover's need."

We'd had our fill, Mack brought our bill, sombrero in his hand,
his shirt was silk, as white as milk, from some far eastern land.

"I have no doubt that when you're out, you'll come back here to dine,
you'll eat the food, get in the mood, your time at home—divine."

A sales receipt, but incomplete, no fortune cookies there,
just a note Confucius wrote, "advice because we care."

"A man and wife should spend their life as all young lovers do,
just make a date to clean your plate at Taco-Fu-Manchu."

A Friend for Life

For anyone having been blessed with the gift—that one friendship based on a chemistry that defies explanation, this poem is for you. I met Robert "Keith" Reed while attending high school in Brandon, Florida in the late 1960s. I don't know what it was that cause us to click. Our friendship continued for over forty years until he was taken away due to illness. During that entire time, we never had a cross word.

Speaking at his funeral was one of the most difficult and cherished things I've ever done. **A Friend for Life** and **Chariots of Thunder** are the results of that friendship and one of the many events we experienced together.

I miss you buddy!

A Friend for Life

I had this friend I came to know when I was but a child,
a friendship started long ago when we were young and wild.

The chemistry we shared was something we did not foresee,
but what fate had in store for us would last an eternity.

My friend was shy and quiet, for attention never fond,
but I was more outgoing and insistent that we bond.

I don't know what I saw in him that made him seem unique,
I hadn't known him long enough to do a real critique.

He had a way about him that so deserved respect
a humor, style and presence that I could not reject.

Our friendship weathered decades, no cross words ever spoken,
a friendship graced with memories to forever be held golden.

Though months or even years might pass without a face-to-face,
a simple note or call would serve to hold our common space.

I always took for granted that our friendship wouldn't end,
but illness came into his life the doctors couldn't mend.

He never knew self-pity, showed no signs of despair,
a trove of grace and spirit even as he lost his hair.

He fought a long, courageous fight, his want so much to stay,
but God had other plans for him and took his soul away.

His funeral was a sad affair despite attempts to quell
the sense of dread and loss I felt as I said my last farewell.

It took some time to read my lines as all there could attest,
my words were spoken from the heart, I gave my very best.

It's hard to capture forty years of memories held so dear,
all spoken with a cracking voice and words all soaked in tears.

I felt so sad to think of just how different life would be,
no more chance to reminisce times shared by him and me.

My friend I think of every day and all the times we shared,
the things life's lessons taught us, the dangers when we dared.

Nothing but my death will let these sacred memories die,
no longer will I need them, there'll be no tears to cry.

Our paths will one day merge again in some celestial place
and give us all the time we need to enjoy our common space.

Little Brother

My younger brother, Donald "Mark" Radford, died of injuries sustained in a motorcycle accident at the age of 48. I was the oldest of four and Mark the second by three years. He and I had significantly different personalities, mine being "laid back" and his being a bit "high-strung." I suppose it was the extreme differences in personalities that separated us as we grew into adults.

Though we failed to see "eye-to-eye" on many fronts, what I loved about him most was his strong sense of family and willingness to do whatever he could to promote their wellbeing. He would literally give the shirt off his back.

He lived for five years in a diminished mental state following the accident. Though physically he looked fine, the severe brain damage he received prevented him from being able to communicate. While being visited one day by our mother, he walked over to a window, looked out and made the perfectly clear statement, "I can't believe this is happening to me." To our knowledge, that was the only intelligible statement he made during the years following the wreck and an indication that for at least that moment, he was aware of the condition he was in.

For no known reason, he went to sleep one night and never woke up. Though we hated losing him, we know he's in a much better place.

Rest in peace little brother.

Little Brother

When our family first began there was only me,
and then my brother came along just after I turned three.

Donald was his given name, but only Mark would do,
so I arranged a title change the day of his debut.

We started out in harmony as friends, just two young boys
who always seemed to get along even sharing each other's toys.

When you're just a little kid, your friendships come and go,
that's when little brother is the dearest friend you know.

My parents said that as a child, I was born at peace,
but in Mark burned a raging fire he never could release.

He always seemed to be at war with demons deep inside,
a battle he would always fight and sometimes couldn't hide.

Our father's love for nature was a common thread he wore,
a love for all God's creatures, a love to be outdoors.

His passion was to travel with just two wheels down below,
the sound of engine's thunder, many miles of open road.

Mark would later take a wife, two daughters they would bear,
a good provider he would be, a deep felt sense of care.

As we grew older things would change—we'd go our separate ways
and never have that brothers' bond to share in later days.

The last chance that we had to speak, when painting was his trade,
he told me of a dream he had, the future's plans he'd laid.

That was only days before a dark fate would befall,
the dreams that he'd confessed to me would not come true at all.

The countryside, a scenic ride with a Harley driver's grin,
a sky of blue, a final cruise, a helmet much too thin.

His chariot of thunder that so many of us feared
would take him on a journey, on a trail of endless tears.

A blink of indecision and a loud and violent crash,
a life of hope and promise was all ended in a flash.

So many lives were shattered on that fateful, tragic day,
so many futures altered, not much to do but pray.

Although he didn't die that day, his injuries—severe,
so much we tried to say to him but knew he couldn't hear.

We couldn't tell how much he knew of the plight that he was in,
he never could communicate just what transpired within.

For years he'd walk a solo path, his eyes—a distant stare,
but all of us who loved him so could sense his deep despair.

A keeper he would always need to help him find his way,
a spirit-free, he'd never be, a life of grave dismay.

He went to sleep one night to fight the demons in his mind
and though he finally won, a lifeless body stayed behind.

Despite our grief, we found relief just knowing he was free,
to feel no pain, a new domain, a better place to be.

My memories of my brother are those when we were boys,
living life in harmony even sharing each other's toys.

Love Child

A fellow member of a writer's group I subscribe to read my poem **Little Brother** and felt compelled to send me a poem she wrote about the loss of her child at the age of eleven months. Her story inspired me and led me to write my own poem **Love Child** as a tribute to her and her son, Brandon. It's written in Sherri's perspective since my view of the experience is through the words she wrote.

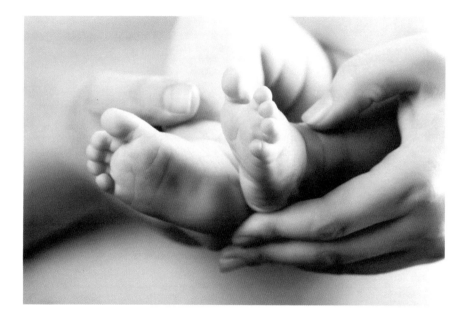

Love Child

A big surprise, to realize I was soon to have a son,
a family new, a life for two, a journey just begun.

Brandon was the name I chose, a handsome man he'll be,
a kindred soul, a heart of gold, a prize for all to see.

The pain of birth, a mother's curse, replaced with tears of joy,
a little angel in my arms, a precious baby boy.

I count his fingers, count the toes on his tiny little feet,
a mother's pride, the joy inside, my life was now complete.

I'd never guessed that I'd be blessed to have him in my life,
to watch him grow, teach all I know, to someday take a wife.

The months just seemed to sail on by, it wasn't quite a year,
I felt that there was something wrong, I could see it in his tears.

Behind the glow, a mother knows, she feels her baby's plight,
a sense that tells what inside dwells, the crying in the night.

I couldn't see how this could be, so innocent and pure,
and while I cried, the doctors tried, but couldn't find a cure.

At night I'd pray and plead by day, can something not be done?
This isn't fair, the pain, despair, please God don't take my son!

You sent this tiny one to me, my sacred task to raise,
but now you want to call him back, you only gave us days.

Oh God, I know your plans for him are holy and divine,
but all I have, I'd gladly give for just a little time.

I knew I had to set him free and let him rise above,
his gift to me his memory and mine his mother's love.

Though time may heal the pain I feel, I'll never be the same,
the precious smile of my love child, Brandon is his name.

The Magnifying Glass

The Magnifying Glass is my attempt to poke fun at a pastime enjoyed by many a young boy (I'll give the girls a pass)—whether he admits it or not! Most inquisitive youngsters eventually discover that a magnifying glass can bring endless hours of destructive pleasure on sunny days. You might want to keep this story out of the hands of your younger kids or at least increase your homeowner's insurance.

The Magnifying Glass

I had a birthday coming and my mom asked what I'd like,
"a catcher's mitt, a stereo, perhaps a brand new bike?"

I thought about it long and hard, my chance had come at last,
I told her what I'd really like is a magnifying glass!

"A magnifying glass", she asked? "That's not much of a toy!
How about some shoes or jeans? You're still a growing boy."

But there behind her puzzled look, I knew that she was proud,
a scientific instrument, not simply something loud.

A gift so educational, a tool to help me learn,
but I could care less how it worked, I had a different yearn.

It's true that things too small to see would be a larger size,
a slimy slug, an ugly bug with a scary mouth and eyes.

The beauty of a butterfly, a flower's pretty bloom,
so many things to greet the eye that needs a little zoom.

But all these silly, girly things were just a bore to me,
'cause I knew what that glass could do, and the fuel it used was free.

I knew that on a sunny day, if I held the glass just right,
I could focus all those useless rays to a tiny spot of light.

A spot so hot that what it touched would soon burst into flames,
no matter what it was before, it'd soon be charred remains.

Any kind of crawly thing that moved a bit too slow,
my magnifying glass and I knew how to make it glow.

I'm glad I couldn't hear them scream, it might have made me sad,
a sunny day meant bug flambé if I was being bad.

After all Buck Rodgers had his gun that shot out rays,
and saber-light by Jedi Knight would stamp out evil ways.

It might not kill space aliens or torch Darth Vader's mug,
but boy my glass can burn the ass off a poor defenseless bug.

My next door neighbor, Billy Smith, was in his yard one day,
he had his magnifying glass and called me out to play.

Bring yours too so me and you can generate more power,
we burned his house right to the ground in just about an hour.

We felt real bad when his mom and dad came home to smoke and ash,
'cause everything they had inside was now reduced to trash.

We tried to act real innocent while the firemen searched for clues,
'til Billy's magnifying glass fell out beside his shoes.

Our cover blown, we should have known it wouldn't be our day,
I'm in my room 'til the next full moon, I can't go out and play.

My magnifying glass is gone, my dad was pretty mad,
no more fun with rays of sun, but I bet the bugs are glad.

A Sailor's Tale

A Sailor's Tale is an adventure/fantasy story set in the mid-1800s involving an ill-fated, oceanic voyage between Scotland and America. It is by far the longest and most challenging piece I've written to date. Containing approximately 2,500 words, A Sailor's Tale was truly a rhyme-fetching experience. I won't give away the "fantasy element," but it's one that's dear to my heart.

Writing the story was a wonderful experience because I felt as though I was actually there during the time I was writing it. You'll have to decide for yourself whether or not the rhyming brings an added depth to the story. It does for me!

A Sailor's Tale

They left the port of Aberdeen in eighteen fifty-three,
a crew of ten courageous men on the good ship Anne Marie.

Of Clipper-class, with triple masts, her colors for the Queen,
a heavy hold of Spanish gold, and tons of British tea.

In command was Herbert Mann, a captain tough as nails,
a driven man with worker's hands, his place below the sails.

"Weigh the anchor, take the helm, we best be underway!
The course is set, we'll head due west and travel twenty days."

Nathan Preen, naïve and green was on his maiden run,
an orphaned teen, his childhood dream, to sail the setting sun.

A spirit high, the daughter's eye, a father's pride and joy,
but Captain Mann won't give her hand to any common boy.

Nate would have to prove his worth, to gain the Captain's trust,
he'd mop the deck and shine the brass, he'd toil from dawn to dusk.

The day the journey first began, the skies were clear and blue,
the ocean calm, the trade winds warm, a pleasure for the crew.

But on day three, a violent sea had touched a blackened sky,
the lookout warned, "A major storm is all that meets the eye!"

Seaman Less had manned the nest, his hope to find a way,
a safer path to avoid the wrath that nature brought that day.

The Captain's call, to brave the squall, "Our cargo must get through!"
Beyond their sight, the storm's sheer might, not noticed by the crew.

They battened hatches, stowed the sails, took refuge down below,
the ship was tossed, direction lost and trouble in the hold.

The Anne Marie was taking sea, her hull so badly cracked,
and all around, a roaring sound, no chance of turning back.

For seven days they'd lose their way, they couldn't navigate,
a shrouding veil of rain and hail, too blind to see their fate.

Seaman Frye was first to die when the sea reclaimed his soul,
whisked away by the salty spray, the storm would take its toll.

By break of day, the storm still raged, for Less the Reaper called,
atop the mast, he'd lost his grasp, a long and fatal fall.

The shrinking crew, now down by two, would struggle through the night,
no time for rest, the final test, they'd not give up the fight.

The mounting cost as more were lost while nature's fury grew,
despite the valiant effort waged, 'twas too much for the crew.

One by one, throughout the night, each man would meet his fate,
when Davy Jones would claim their bones, except for Mann and Nate.

As Nathan tried, the Captain cried, "Abandon ship you must,"
take my daughter as your wife, you've earned her father's trust.

Captain Mann, with rope in hand, a sacrifice to be,
the knot he tied for his final ride to the bottom of the sea.

Nathan grabbed the Captain's hand, he couldn't let him die.
"The Anne Marie, my grave will be", the Captain yelled with pride!

He did his best to reach the nest, his telescope in hand,
a distant shore not there before, he cried out "I see land!"

A sandy beach, just out of reach was coming into view,
but not before a jagged shore would break the ship in two.

Her deck had slipped below the waves, the Anne Marie was lost,
his mates were gone, he was all alone, he'd pay the final cost.

The ship was listing hard to port, so tired, he lost his hold,
she cast him free, to hit the sea and the salty depths below.

Headed towards the ocean's floor with no more will to fight,
upon his shirt, a gentle jerk, then up towards the light.

He hardly sensed his fast ascent so weak from lack of sleep,
was it God's own helping hand that plucked him from the deep?

A day would pass before he'd wake up lying in the sand,
fresh air to breath, no memory of how he reached dry land.

Rolling over on his back, he gazed upon the sky,
the warming sun, no damage done, so happy he'd survived.

Bruised and weak, but on his feet, he took a look around,
in search for food and water too, whatever could be found.

He scaled the islands highest point to get a better view,
just rocks and sand, a barren land, provisions very few.

Just beyond the rocky shore, a ship there used to be,
so few remains, a tattered sail and pieces of debris.

That's when Nate first sensed his fate, his chances looking bleak,
no food, no water anywhere, he wouldn't last a week.

The days went by, then three and four, he felt the end was near,
to never see his love again was Nathan's greatest fear.

Came day five, though still alive, his body growing frail,
but near the beach, within his reach, a sight his eyes beheld.

A seaweed basket filled with food just floating with the tide,
a turtle shell, fresh water filled, so thankful, Nate just cried.

But were his eyes just telling lies, or could this truly be?
The trembling hand of a desperate man, he plucked them from the sea.

So real indeed, he quenched his need, then paused and chanted grace,
this island home, not his alone, "My friend, please show your face!"

His stomach stuffed, he ate so much, some needed weight to gain,
a chance to wash his beard and locks, for now, his life sustained.

This sacred gift, he'd find adrift, the same place every day,
his gratitude for drink and food, but who the debt to pay?

One night late, he lay in wait, his desperate hope to see,
just who it was that always came to tend his every need.

Lying still in the nighttime chill a stirring sound he'd hear,
amazed was he, for soon he'd see a woman would appear.

With skin so fair, long blonde hair and eyes of sultry blue,
though void of clothes, her locks that flowed would hide some parts from view.

Quietly, he tried to hide, but just as he had feared,
a falling stone, his presence known, with a splash she disappeared.

Nathan peered, the water clear, no trace, just waves and foam,
she left no sign, no way to find the place that she called home.

Nate was sure the maiden's lair would have to be close by,
he'd scouted most of the island's coast, but saw no place to hide.

He'd not explored the northern shore, steep cliffs and crashing waves,
to scale the rocks, no shoes or socks, a task he'd failed to brave.

He'd rest the night, at morning's light his journey would begin,
the risk of life, a willing price, this mystery had to end.

For half the day he made his way, so cautiously he tread,
the searing heat, his bloodied feet, a trail of scarlet red.

He paused to take a needed break, the pain by now severe,
but came along, a mournful song, to captivate his ear.

He couldn't understand the words, but had no real desire,
as the penetrating melody just set his soul afire.

Along the coast, he chased the notes to learn from whence they came,
he'd lost control of his heart and soul, like a moth that's drawn to flame.

Now the sound was growing strong, his journey near the end,
high atop the jagged rocks, around the final bend.

There below, a quiet cove with a waterfall and spring,
the water's edge, a mossy ledge, a beauty lay and sing.

Above her waist, an angel's face, so pretty and petite,
but shocked he be for now he'd see she had no legs or feet.

What did begin as supple skin below had turned to scales,
and where her legs and feet would be, he saw a fish's tail!

But even though what he beheld had come as a surprise,
tales of lore he'd heard before, he'd written off as lies.

Stories told by sailors old, who'd sailed around the world,
described a creature—half a fish, the other half a girl.

The reputation Mermaids had was running ships aground,
distracting even veteran crews with hypnotizing sounds.

Nathan knew it wasn't true, without her he'd be dead,
her thankless deed, to meet his needs, to make sure he was fed.

The only thing that mattered now, he had to bring her near,
to win her trust, to let her know, of him she should not fear.

Cloaked by darkness, down the rocks, he softly made his way,
to reach the ledge at water's edge before she swam away.

Mission bound, without a sound, so silently he crept,
'cause just below, so very close, a dreaming beauty slept.

So afraid his pounding heart would compromise his plan,
she'd not escape, for as she slept, he'd grab her by the hand.

An arm around his rocky perch, the other hanging free,
some slippery moss, poor Nate was tossed headfirst into the sea.

Dropping past the sleeping lass, the ledge would break his fall,
and down he went, his body limp, he couldn't move at all.

A second splash, a gentle grasp, blue eyes and long blonde hair,
as once again a helping hand would bring him up for air.

In her arms and safe from harm, a mossy bed she made,
and pressed a sponge against his head in hopes his pain would fade.

Dazed and weak, he couldn't speak, just satisfied to breathe,
to let her tend, a chance to mend, so glad she didn't leave.

He looked into her eyes of blue, his own reflection there,
an injured man, he raised his hand and gently touched her hair.

A sudden sense of self-defense, her tendency to flee.
"Oh please don't go, I need you so!" she heard poor Nathan plea.

She felt his fear, his voice sincere, and by his side she'd stay,
a man so hurt, she'd not desert, make sure he'd be okay.

Her natural skill for fixing ills, the like he'd never seen,
his wounds she'd treat, his head and feet, to him she was a queen.

While he healed, she brought him meals and gave him tender care,
with sharpened shell, his whiskers fell and then she trimmed his hair.

The words he spoke, though very few, she seemed to understand,
but no reply except a smile and gestures with her hands.

His wounds now gone and feeling strong, a happy man was he,
to him it seemed, he shared a dream with an angel from the sea.

The happy times he'd get to leave his isle of rock and sand,
to tour her world, a boy and girl would swim off hand in hand.

The chance to see what lie beneath, a world so rich and vast,
he'd hold on tight and enjoy the sights, that girl could swim so fast!

She taught him how to hold his breath, to stay beneath the waves,
a deep inhale, but still he'd fail to have enough to save.

When they'd dare get far from air, so far they couldn't swim,
she'd softly press her lips to his and pass some air to him.

Always close to Nate she'd be, for him her heart so fond,
but not to dare a love affair, no everlasting bond.

So close they grew, but they both knew their love could never be,
between a man who lived on land and a creature of the sea.

Some nights late, he'd lie awake and hear her mournful song,
her heart in pain and tears like rain would fall the whole night long.

The pain she felt was his as well and at times he'd cry alone,
their internal flame was all in vain, his need—to get back home.

As weeks went by, he'd sit and sigh and think of times before,
his mind would roam to the girl back home on a far off distant shore.

He couldn't help but wonder if he'd ever see the day,
when another splendid sailing ship by chance might come his way.

A year had passed since he left that mast of the good ship Ann Marie,
and just like then, the warm trade winds brought a dark and violent sea.

A fearsome sight with lightning strikes, hard rain and pounding hail,
while Nate was safe in a coastal cave, on the sea he spied a sail!

A lonely ship that would rise and dip, being tossed from wave to wave,
a distracted crew with much to do for they had a ship to save.

Nate could tell from her bellowed sails that soon she'd pass on by,
but to swim that fast, he would never last, still he knew he had to try.

To hesitate would seal his fate so he chose to leave dry land,
and there she'd be, from beneath the sea, to take him by the hand.

It made her grieve to know he'd leave but she had to let him go,
to keep him there would not be fair, she truly loved him so.

Out to sea at mermaid's speed, as the wind and ocean roared,
once in view of a wide-eyed crew, one cried, "Man overboard!"

They threw a rope, on the end a float, with a splash it hit close by,
then a salty kiss for the man she'd miss, in tears she waved goodbye.

Soaking wet, but safe on deck, the questions came his way,
"You're still alive! How did you survive?" Young Nathan wouldn't say.

Aberdeen was a festive scene for a man they thought was dead,
and the very next spring, he gave a ring to the girl he'd planned to wed.

He'd live his life with a sailor's wife, more adventures there would be,
but none so dear as the one that year back in eighteen fifty three.

In years of late, when old man Nate had consumed his share of ale,
the kids in town would gather 'round to hear an old sailor's tale.

The one loved best, more than all the rest, was the time he was lost at sea,
when his life was spared by a maiden fair from the wreck of the Anne Marie.

The Beach

My family moved from Texas to central Florida just prior to me entering the sixth grade. At that age, perhaps the most significant benefit of living in Florida was its many miles of sugar-sand beach. There's just something magical about the ocean with its vastness and constant state of motion. But for me, being of very fair complexion, the beach scene had an unfortunate side effect that could make visits there a bit less than palatable—especially after the fact.

Out of the thirteen years I lived in Florida, I can't recall a single one that I didn't spend at least a day or two in misery as my body would attempt to heal itself after being "nuked" during a beach visit.

Despite the misery I regularly experienced, every new summer brought the warming of the Gulf waters and an unavoidable urge to head back for a day of "fun in the sun." I would never remember the bad stuff from the prior year, so I'd head out for another day of solar exposure. "Surfs up!"

The Beach

'Twas finally here, that time of year we most looked forward to,
the warming rays of summer days and cloudless skies of blue.

The sun shone bright, the time just right to head out for the beach,
what we liked most, the Florida coast was right within our reach.

A drive not far in the family car, just an hour or so away,
a chance to be with the sand and sea, what a place to spend the day!

The cooler filled to keep things chilled and dad in the driver's seat,
we left our abode and hit the road for a most enjoyable treat.

But the old-folks there with silver hair slowed traffic to a crawl,
in part to blame, just a single lane, not a chance to pass at all.

It seemed the town was all beach-bound and the clock just ticked away,
the beach so near, but now our fear—we'd have no time to play!

Then at last, dad hit the gas and we left those jerks behind,
I gazed outside as we passed on by, leaving gestures most unkind.

Once we got to the parking lot, was a sea of smoking tar,
and the searing heat on our tender feet made the trot seem way too far.

A relief to land on a patch of sand where the pain would soon subside,
then to take a stroll in the ocean's shoal of the soft receding tide.

Above the shore the seagulls soared as they danced the breeze with grace,
though a few might swoop and drop some poop on a gazer's hair or face.

I'd always heard, just a stupid bird in an act of circumstance,
but it wasn't true, I was sure they knew—too precise to be by chance.

Their beady eyes would tell no lies—those birds weren't fooling me,
that rolling surf was their home turf and they loved to watch us flee.

Along the way, all the tourists lay and their unprotected skin
had begun to show a fluorescent glow, I just couldn't help but grin.

They chose to bare, but I've been there and trust me it ain't fun,
for soon they'd dread that shade of red, 'cause a burn can't be undone.

In a pool they'll sleep as blisters leak and their skin begins to peel,
that leper-look, 'cause man they're cooked, the pain they're soon to feel!

About that time I'd come to find that all my sound advice,
I'd failed to heed, so now I'd need to pack myself with ice.

Bleached-white hair and complexion fair, I guessed I'd never learn,
the choice I made to avoid the shade, a guarantee I'd burn.

None too soon came the afternoon and time to head on back,
for an itchy ride, a toasted hide and sand in every crack.

I'd then recall my thoughts last fall on my last beach-day return,
the season's end and a need to mend, but a lesson still not learned.

The beach and me would not agree on a painless-fun event,
the sun, the heat, all the blistered meat and recovery time I spent.

But the price I'd pay for the fun that day would fade from memory,
so I'd be back for a sand-packed crack and burns in the third degree.

The Bench

The setting for **The Bench** is the backyard of my home in north Georgia. Being a lover of nature, my wife asked me to clear a small spot in the woods behind our house where she could escape the rigors of daily life—to enjoy a quiet moment of solitude.

After clearing the spot, we had to secure a most befitting perch upon which she could bask and reflect.

During the warm months of spring and summer, her silhouette can often be seen partially obscured by the foliage, sitting quietly in **the bench**.

The Bench

As darkness fades to light of day, a mother and her fawn,
you just might see behind the trees there grazing on our lawn.

To see or hear a fox or deer, or other timid guest,
those hungry words from baby birds beneath their mother's breast.

Above, a sound, then on the ground, majestic birds of prey,
a hungry brood, they search for food, the chipmunks hide away.

An owl we'll see, or two or three, both parents and a child,
a huge wingspan, a sight so grand, all beauties of the wild.

My lover's plan, a spot of land, a quiet place to be,
where she'd behold all nature's gold, a space that's worry-free.

The benefit, a place to sit, so close but oh so far,
a place to pray, a world away, obscured from human's scar.

A site serene in forest green, where she could just reflect,
a mental state, to meditate, life's troubles she'd neglect.

A path I'd make, a walk to take, a little overgrown,
remove the weeds, the final need, a most befitting throne.

A bench to find, the rustic kind, of wood and metal cast,
a seat to blend and not offend, one guaranteed to last.

The likes we'd spy in a store nearby, a garden bench we'd find,
the perfect fit for a place to sit, to leave her cares behind.

Just yards away from stress of day, so lush with forest dew,
rustling leaves, a gentle breeze, to read a book or two.

Enjoyment brief, for like a thief, no warmth of summer of sun,
the forest scene, no longer green when old man winter comes.

That sacred place will change its face as summer fades away,
for soon the trees would have no leaves, no creatures come to play.

Until the spring, no birds will sing, no sign of life around,
the winter days, no grass to graze, a hard and frozen ground.

At last the thaw will come to draw all nature from its sleep,
as none too soon, the plants will bloom and vines begin their creep.

Just like before, the forest floor will thicken, green and new,
again to grace this special place and hide the bench from view.

And once again this spot of land, all furnished for my queen,
her place to be alone and free, encased in forest green.

The Soldier

I wrote **The Soldier** just before Memorial Day 2011. During these times of war, we're often presented with images of our troops heading out—or returning from the battlefield. Being a frequent traveler, I'm constantly reminded of these patriots who sacrifice so much making their contribution to our nation's security. It seems as though hardly a week goes by that the biography of a fallen soldier isn't covered on the nightly news.

It's impossible to appreciate the terrors these men and women often face in the execution of their duties, or the profound changes in peoples' lives both at home and abroad that result.

I was on a flight recently with a young soldier wearing a tee shirt that bore the words, "When the smoke clears, if I feel pain—I know I'm still alive." Both of his legs were prosthetic. **The Soldier** is about valor and sacrifice.

The Soldier

Long before, in times of war, an able-bodied male
would have no voice to make the choice, he'd serve or go to jail.

But times have changed, they're not the same as those of yesteryear,
unlike before, to go to war one has to volunteer.

Their own free will, to die or kill, defend their flag with pride,
to sacrifice and not think twice, to take it all in stride.

Daughter, sons, they look so young, yet fearlessly they go,
and they'll engage as battles rage, a terror few will know.

Everyday they're in harm's way, they tread on dangerous ground,
unwanted guests, explosive vests or a hidden sniper's round.

A barren land of rock and sand, they sit prepared to fight,
in holes they lay 'till heat of day replaces chill of night.

They'll not complain, they don't seek fame, a mission to complete,
a wrong to right, a war to fight, a foe they must defeat.

The arms they bear, of high-tech fare, on land, in air and space,
they'll take their toll by remote control, an assault without a face.

But in the towns where danger's found, they'll take it to the street,
with gun in hand, they make their stand, not knowing who they'll meet.

Eye to eye, they'll fight and die, civilians they'll defend,
though fight they must, they'll win the trust, not enemy, but friend.

They'll not neglect a child or pet, the innocents so dear,
they'll render aid, "don't be afraid, you have no need to fear."

Common views on the nightly news, returning troops enjoy
applause, the cheers and prideful tears, too soon they'll redeploy.

They're glad to see their family but always on their mind,
those out of site, still in the fight—the friends they left behind.

Some will claim a hero's fame but we won't hear them brag,
for they'll return by way of urn or a box wrapped in a flag.

A solemn scene, a mother's scream, a sight profoundly sad,
a wife will mourn, a child just born will never meet its dad.

It just might be that those who feel the greatest loss of all,
were there that night to share the fight and saw their comrade fall.

The pain they feel will never heal, the soldier's lifelong hell,
for every year they'll shed a tear and toast the ones who fell.

While here at home, debates go on, their mission second-guessed,
agendas staged as war is waged, we sacrifice our best.

Some of those who live by prose have never had to fight.
They'll pass a bill on Capitol Hill then home by Friday night.

The gift they'll give to those who live, a life they can't restart,
if valor's shone with flesh and bone, perhaps a purple heart.

Some will stay in God's embrace, the only prize they'll claim,
a special day at the end of May and a cross that bears their name.

As long as man shall rule the land and choose to disagree,
the soldier's call—to save us all and keep our nation free.

They'll show no fear and volunteer, they know what they must do,
to fight and die with colors high, the red, the white and blue.

Treasured Chest

Several years ago, my lovely wife Gloria was diagnosed with breast cancer. After a year of surgeries, chemotherapy, radiation therapy, needles and scans, she was given the green light to proceed with reconstruction that included a little size increase. During a brief consultation with the surgeon, an agreement was reached as to what that "size" would be.

Following the procedure, she awoke to discover the plan had been "adjusted up" in the interest of anatomical perfection.

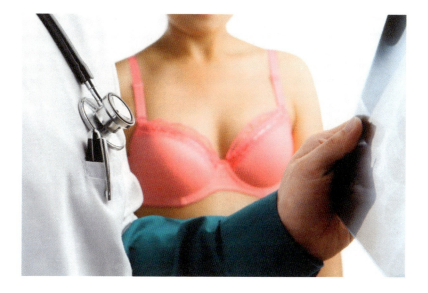

Treasured Chest

I believe when God made Eve, he had a special plan,
her body-style was meant for child, not just for sake of man.

Upon her chest, he hung a breast and then he made it two,
a balanced pair was only fair 'cause one just wouldn't do.

A simple tool for needed fuel, so after every nap,
by way of boob, her baby's food would always be on tap.

The grand design would work just fine, a source of nutriment,
to meet a need, her child to feed, the plan was heaven sent.

But soon the plan got out of hand and man became obsessed,
when he'd surmise the proper size, that big was always best.

The likely cause, their tiny paws when nursing was the game,
a ratio as hands would grow but boobs would stay the same.

Women kind would often find their natural gift too shy
of what it'd take, for nature's sake, to snare a handsome guy.

They'd need a lure to help insure they stood out from the rest,
a shadow cast by larger flasks, some large protruding breasts.

And so began a great demand, a new cosmetic trade,
the less endowed—the flatter crowd could now have new ones made.

Surgery was all they'd need to grow a size or two,
and some were sold on going bold - where only huge would do.

The trend would deem that self-esteem be based too much on size,
but only souls are made of gold, the boobs were not the prize.

Despite how smart or pure of heart a woman proved to be,
for shallow men with thoughts of sin, the boobs were all they'd see.

But big or small, the crucial call, a task they'd best attend,
a test to take for safety's sake, for what might lurk within.

A self-exam and mammogram would show the coast was clear,
or might detect a slight defect—a woman's greatest fear.

A lump might be too small to see, but quickly grow—it might,
then cause despair and loss of hair, a long and dreadful fight.

My lovely bride took such a ride, a trek we all would share,
a surgeon's knife, a year of strife, a heavy load to bear.

She took it well and few could tell the pain she felt inside,
synthetic hair so none would stare, she took it all in stride.

All along, a spirit strong, from work she'd take no leave,
she'd take no break for pity's sake or even time to grieve.

Needle-bound, the chemo-lounge with other patients—brave,
where bodies sip a toxic drip, the poison meant to save.

Years would pass and then, at last, she'd get the doc's release,
no longer sore, a full restore and little size increase.

Nothing grand, a modest plan, perhaps a bigger "B,"
to our surprise, he'd supersize, "You Dolly? Pardon me!"

His work—the best, a treasured chest, a most impressive suite,
but looking down, she'd see no ground or either of her feet.

Her morning's stress, she picks her dress, her modesty intact,
a task to do, to hide from view, a now much larger rack.

I'm sure in time she'll be just fine with her new silhouette,
no longer care about the stares, the compliments she'll get.

The French profess the perfect breast—sheer size will not define,
as best in class would fill a glass that's made for drinking wine.

But everywhere except for there, a different rule applies,
'cause men don't care, they'll always stare, it's all about the size.

The Mirror

Lifting weights has been a lifelong passion of mine since my early twenties. As is the case for many, it's a passion driven more by a sense of need than one of actual enjoyment. I'm a firm believer that the key to a healthy life is consistent exercise. I would also include diet, but mine is quite atrocious.

I learned early on that perhaps the most significant tool found in a gym is not an exercise machine, a set of weights or pair of dumbbells. Nope, the most important tool in the gym is the mirror. Without the mirror, a would-be body builder would have no way to gauge his improvement or perfect his form. But more importantly, without the mirror to constantly shower him with silent compliments, he might not muster the motivation to continue his pursuit of physical excellence.

Besides, if one looks hard enough and stands in the perfect light, he might catch a glimpse of an image seen only by him. By the way, when I say "him," I mean "him/her," but it looks dumb to present it that way—so I just say "him" for short. Sorry, ladies!

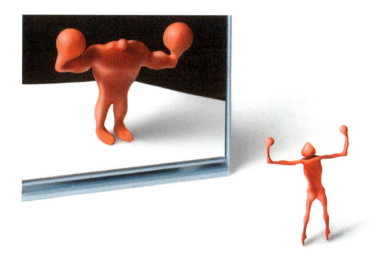

The Mirror

I'll not regret the smell of sweat and sound of clanking plates,
the grunts and strain, the muscle pain—the joy of lifting weights.

At twenty-two, the thing to do was pretty clear to me,
a good routine to keep me lean—my personal decree.

The perfect age to set the stage for staying really fit,
a driven man, a lifelong plan I swore I'd never quit.

A membership and daily trip, my means for getting strong,
to share my dream, the office team would also come along.

There we'd meet, right up the street where body builders go,
and once we met, we'd toil and sweat to make our muscles grow.

That little gym that we'd attend had mildew-stained décor
and mirrors tall on every wall, from the ceiling to the floor.

Few would pass that shiny glass without a lifter's stance,
a pose or two to see what grew since last they took a glance.

But mirrors there could bring despair if the image they'd reflect
was life supine, a love to dine and physical neglect.

To stand just right in perfect light, inhale to shrink their gut,
and squeeze their cheeks to look more sleek, to hide that sagging butt.

Some came in so frail and thin to grow by lifting weights,
attempts so far with just a bar, in time they'd add some plates.

After five the place would thrive but very few would stay,
they'd drop on in for five or ten then head for the buffet.

Over time I'd come to find the gym was not my scene,
'twas more I'd dub a social club than people getting lean.

A better way to start my day—I'd build a gym at home,
convenience sake, to stay in shape without the need to roam.

A private space, the perfect place that's built for only me,
to meditate by way of plates and solitarily.

Years before, I know I swore I'd work out 'til I die,
so far – so good, just like I should—most every day I try.

Though at the start, a stronger heart and youth were on my side,
I've now been plagued with signs of age I've learned to take in stride.

An older frame, I can't maintain the weight I used to lift,
unlike before, I'm always sore, old age is not a gift.

My muscle mass ain't hard as brass, no love for nuts and grains,
but thanks to lard, now all that's hard are arteries and veins.

Ain't no fun to take a run—I much prefer the Gym,
machines and weights define my fate, they'll keep my body trim.

A manly cave is what I crave with fitness gear galore,
some cool AC, a rock CD and carpet on the floor.

Mirrors spaced about the place reflect a man at work,
to self-critique, refine technique, expose where fat may lurk.

Perhaps I'm vain, but just the same, I have to have a gauge,
a driving force to stay on course—to help me turn the page.

A look into another's view that might escape my eye,
a chance to see what others see, the mirrors never lie.

It's on my list, I seldom miss the morning workout call,
the place to be, just room for me and mirrors wall to wall.

The Runt

The Runt is based on a well-known short story entitled **No Charge for Love** (author unknown). I found the story so inspirational that I had to write a poem around it. Being a dog lover, this is one of my personal favorites. Be prepared to shed a happy tear!

The Runt

Father Dan, a holy man had a little patch of ground
and a modest place he shared with Grace, in a quiet little town.

With Grace, his wife, he'd shared his life, his bride of fifty years,
they made their way on preacher's pay, they were always in arrears.

A payment made in the form of trade, a dog would come their way,
a one-year old with fur of gold, they named her Molly May.

Father Dan had visions grand of getting Molly bred,
and then her brood he'd sell for food to keep his family fed.

A friend agreed, to meet their need he'd offer up his stud,
a handsome male that had never failed, from a line of royal blood.

The moon was bright that Friday night when Molly's puppies came,
the Labrador gave birth to four that all looked just the same.

But number five had almost died, not healthy like the rest,
so small and weak, her future bleak, a stunted growth at best.

Some special care, but no repair, the vet did all he could,
defects at birth reduced her worth, a fact they understood.

But they agreed they'd wait and see if maybe she'd survive,
so very frail, a cooked tail and very small in size.

They prayed with love and from above a miracle was sent,
Grace and Dan would nurse by hand, her death they'd circumvent.

They named her Meg, a defective leg insured she'd never run,
as the others played, behind she stayed to bask in the morning sun.

In time she'd grow, but traveled slow—had trouble keeping up,
from the very start, a giant heart, just a happy little pup.

Weeks went by and the time arrived to put them up for sale,
a poster made and then displayed, they hoped it wouldn't fail.

The poster said, "They're thoroughbred and healthy as can be.
With fur of gold, just eight weeks old, you must come by and see."

Back from town, they'd settled down, been running 'round the clock,
they thought it best to take a rest when they heard a gentle knock.

Tones of Emotion

At the door, not seen before, there stood a little guy
with tattered clothes, a dirty nose and oh, so very shy.

"Mama read what your poster said and I had to come and see,
to get a friend with time to spend, a friend to play with me.

He knew their means from the worn-out jeans and his shirt tied in a knot,
Said, "Son, you see, those pups aren't free, I'm afraid they cost a lot."

An excited smile from an anxious child, he opened up his hand,
his fingers filled with a dollar bill wrapped up in a rubber band.

"Sir, I worked real hard to clean the yard, mom gave me all she had,
money's rare, not much to spare ever since we lost my dad.

"Well, just today you can stay and play and that won't cost a dime,"
then through the door, he could see all four, he would have the grandest time.

The pups were glad to see the lad, they could lick his face all day,
then came the runt, she limped out front to join the rest at play.

When he saw that pup, he picked her up and held her to his chest,
with an instant glow, he said, "I know, of the bunch this one's the best!"

"The small female is not for sale, she can't run or chase a ball,
when you take a ride, she can't run alongside, she'd be no fun at all."

The little man just looked a Dan and as clear as he could be,
he said, "Yes I know, she moves real slow, but that's okay with me."

He grabbed the seam of his tattered jeans and pulled it up his leg,
said he understood as only he could, what it meant to be like Meg.

Dan could see, where a leg should be was an artificial limb,
and his little shoe, he could see right through, it was custom-made for him.

Father Dan, with a trembling hand and his eyes all welled with tears,
knelt down low to be real close to a boy of seven years.

He whispered, "Son, God's work is done, it's a sign I must attend,
she's yours to take, a pair you'll make, she'll be your special friend."

Time to go, with little Meg in tow he slowly walked away
while hand in hand, Grace looked at Dan and said, "What a splendid day!"

The Western

The Western was inspired by my love for western movies, particularly the ones of vintage fare. Their plots, though often simple and predicable, were always based on good values and high morality. The storyline pitted good against evil and the good guys almost always won. The characters were larger than life and the cinematography usually spectacular. **The Western** is a story that consolidates the plots of a many old western movies. It makes me wonder if maybe the same person wrote them all!

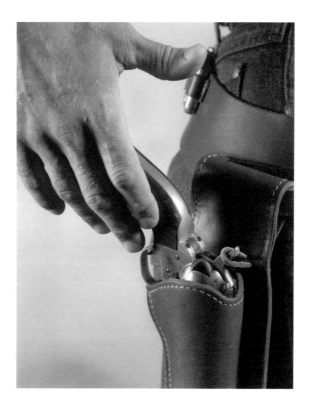

The Western

A common theme on the silver screen and the one I love the best,
is the classic fight between wrong and right in the days of the wild, wild west.

Famous names like Ford and Wayne, we knew they'd never fail,
an endless lust for what was just and justice would prevail.

As words would scroll, the story told would bring us up to date,
and set the stage so any age would know just who to hate.

Beginning scenes showed fields of green and miles of cloudless sky,
the sun would blaze as cattle grazed in the shade of mountains high.

Was so pristine, or so it seemed, but high above the town,
a baron there made sure despair was always raining down.

Within his view was a farm or two where others worked the land,
but all he saw was a pending flaw in his most ambitious plan.

A violent course with no remorse, he'd seal his neighbors' fate,
his only spoil was blood-stained soil, and a lock on heaven's gate.

A brutal man, he'd steal their land or buy it for a song,
they'd sign their deed to quench his greed, they had to go along.

To save the lives of kids and wives, they'd leave their farms behind,
a lawless land for the common man, the justice there was blind.

Across the plains were signs of flames where rustlers did their work,
with iron in hand, they'd change a brand, abound did evil lurk.

The open fire where they'd retire would keep the chill at bay,
then they'd awake, more stock to take, despair seemed there to stay.

The baron's men were helping him to build a massive herd,
and those who knew of things they'd do would never say a word.

They lacked the might to stand and fight, they'd face the baron's court,
a gun for hire in dark attire who loved to kill for sport.

A heartless man, a hired hand who was always dressed in black,
a six-gun pair was what he'd wear and he'd shoot you in the back.

When first he came and said his name, the folks knew what he had done,
the men he'd killed for a dollar bill and the few he'd killed for fun.

Was such despair when he was there, not a soul would take a stand,
for they all knew how fast he drew, not one would lend a hand.

His name "Black Bart," he'd wield his art as a means to intimidate,
whenever near, they'd all stand clear, a man they learned to hate.

The local law would never draw, he'd take the baron's pay,
when townsfolk cried, he closed his eyes or looked the other way.

But in the end, these desperate men would gather in the dark,
and draft a plan to hire a man with a faster draw than Bart.

The man they'd seek to save the meek would wear a hat of white.
He'd don a skill—the means to kill and for cash he'd lead the fight.

He rode a steed of stately breed, his saddle trimmed in studs,
above him sat a Stetson hat to match his fancy duds.

A Pistol graced his slender waist with a handle made of pearl,
though all the men would bow to him, he'd only bow to girls.

A handsome face, such style and grace, and always so polite,
a steady hand, a lady's man with the valor of a knight.

But baron's smart and void of heart, he did his homework well,
he found at last, a checkered past our hero didn't tell.

Long before, the hat he wore had not been colored white,
he's served some time for doing crime, a desperado's plight.

Our heroine would then begin to doubt our hero's fame,
but soon she'd learn, his life he'd turned and so restored his name.

Now and then the macho men would trade a threat or two,
but in good time, we knew we'd find them standing shoe to shoe.

Time would pass until at last the duelers' stage was set,
and then at noon in a grand saloon onlookers placed their bets.

While on the street, the two would meet and stare each other down,
prepared to fight, both black and white—the fastest guns in town.

On either side, the folks would hide, their hearts all filled with hope,
then guns would clash with muzzle flash and the pungent smell of smoke.

The lesser man with a slower hand would soil his fancy duds
and learn defeat when he hit the street in a pool of crimson mud.

The folks in town would gather around a body lying still,
a bloody mess with a new address—a hole upon Boot Hill.

Our man in white had won the fight, but the job was still not done,
the baron's men would not defend against our hero's gun.

The sheriff there would never dare to uphold his tainted crown,
he'd mount his horse and set a course, then gallop out of town.

He'd not get far before his star would grace our hero's chest,
and with his draw, enforce the law, he'd prove to be the best.

The deed was done by way of gun with a handle made of pearl,
the town would mend and in the end, our hero got the girl!

Cyber Date

I have a few friends who've played the Internet dating game. Some had excellent results—others not so. I think it all has to do with how honest the entrants are when it comes to filling out their personal profiles. I wouldn't be surprised to learn that on a few occasions folks might be a little less than honest.

In Cyber Date, two lonely people desperate for love embellish their "attributes" in hopes of finding that special person.

Cyber Date

A fellow named Stan was a real homely man, but also a kind, decent guy,
a true social drone who lived all alone and was known for his being quite shy.

"A real boring life," said a friend and his wife, "the man's never been on a date,
he keeps to himself with his heart on a shelf, what the man really needs is a mate!"

His one greatest fear, the rejection he'd hear—one thing he was certain about,
his appearance was bleak so his chances were weak that a lady would ever go out.

His laugh had a sound like an old basset hound that was howling so loud at the moon,
and his high-pitched voice was an excellent choice for a character in a cartoon.

It didn't look good that he'd date like he should, he was always self-conscious of looks,
but he handled his tears and his deep-seated fears by immersing himself in his books.

An ad that he'd seen in a sports magazine touted services wrought with success,
for a fairly small bill and a form he would fill with some details he'd have to confess.

His big chance at last and a way he could cast a new image that no one could see,
some traits he would list with a very slight twist using keys on his office PC.

His own profile page would then set the stage, to serve as the finest of bait,
a bright shiny lure and bound, he was sure, to find him the most perfect mate.

A real painful task, the questionnaire asked him for details that didn't feel right,
it seemed pretty clear that if he was sincere, he wouldn't get one single bite.

The last thing he'd want was a picture in front, a mug shot that he couldn't hide,
for most in a dress, it would only distress and could even make small children cry.

They wanted to know of his shape—head to toe, not the best light that he could be in,
but he used lots of Nair to remove all the hair from his knuckles, back, belly and chin.

A bit plump and bald, he wasn't that tall, but in text he'd embellish a bit,
an inch here and there, after all—who would care? The uglier parts he'd omit.

His big Hobbit feet were a bit less than sheik in the open-toed sandals he wore,
when he tried to secure a complete pedicure, they hurriedly showed him the door.

His skin pale and white, like he came out at night, he would edit a bit to enhance,
his task at an end, he hit the word "send"—his last step to finding romance.

Days would go by and he'd get no reply from the profile containing his boast,
then when surfing one day, good luck came his way in the form of an interesting post.

A lady named Joyce was seeking a choice and used the same service as Stan,
a sexy young lass who was known to have class, she was searching the Net for a man.

The profile she sent, though sincerity meant, just promoted her positive traits,
some details she missed had not made the list, for like Stan, she was casting out bait.

The photo enclosed had failed to disclose any features except for her smile,
but he wouldn't reject what he couldn't inspect, at the meeting he'd just reconcile.

She was caught in his net, the date was all set at a little café down the street
where so very soon during lunchtime at noon was the girl he was destined to meet.

He raced for the place at a spirited pace while not knowing if she'd even show,
for maybe a bloke was just playing a joke, with email you don't really know.

The first to arrive, he sashayed inside and secured them a table for two,
then he stared at the door in hopes he would score, he didn't know what else to do.

A list he'd prepared from the emails they shared was a menu for how she should look,
he checked every trait as he searched for his date and a meeting he'd never forget.

He sat in his chair with a most anxious stare as the single young ladies appeared,
not one did he miss but not one matched his list, a no-show was just what he feared.

From his seat he could see the head Maître d' with a guest who was looking his way,
a woman of sorts wearing Bermuda shorts - it couldn't be her! No way!"

Her profile would state she had low body-weight and a head full of lovely red hair,
but what met his eye looked a bit like a guy who even had use for his Nair.

She'd not give him fits, but her legs and her pits showed she favored a "natural" style,
and so short was she, eye-to-eye they would be but she did have a beautiful smile.

Her "tiny physique" was a tad bit unique, a model she never would be,
she hadn't been graced with a beautiful face, but then of course neither had he.

Her claimed "big blue eyes" were a bit small in size or maybe they just looked that way
through glasses so thick that she couldn't see Dick who was standing a few feet away.

He rose to his feet with a gentleman's greet, and thanked her for joining him there,
some small talk to make as they waited for steak while neither could help but to stare.

As they both could see, things purported to be were not necessarily fact,
that guilty were they, neither willing to say what was true, but to put on an act.

Both would confess as the lunch date progressed until very few secrets remained,
and so it did seem that the hopes and the dreams of the two were exactly the same.

Chewing his meat, Stan had started to speak when a big piece got stuck in his throat,
and his failure to clear led to panic and fear being sure that was all that she wrote.

His look of despair as he struggled for air convinced Joyce that she needed to act,
the choice that she made was to jump to his aid and get him the air that he lacked.

While Stanley just wheezed, she gave him a squeeze until the obstruction was clear,
but still headed south, she gave mouth to mouth until danger was no longer near.

Stan was impressed and feeling so blessed as he thanked her for saving his life,
then down on one knee like he'd seen on TV, he asked her if she'd be his wife.

Of course, she'd accept as both of them wept, a moment that Hallmark would treasure,
and neither would miss living life filled with bliss and joy that no mortal could measure.

Two homely souls with hearts made of gold and appearances preferably hid,
a new family tree might be painful to see, so hopefully they won't have a kid.

A bond that began from an Internet plan had led to a grand wedding day
and honeymoon night that would turn out just right because beauty's a light switch away!